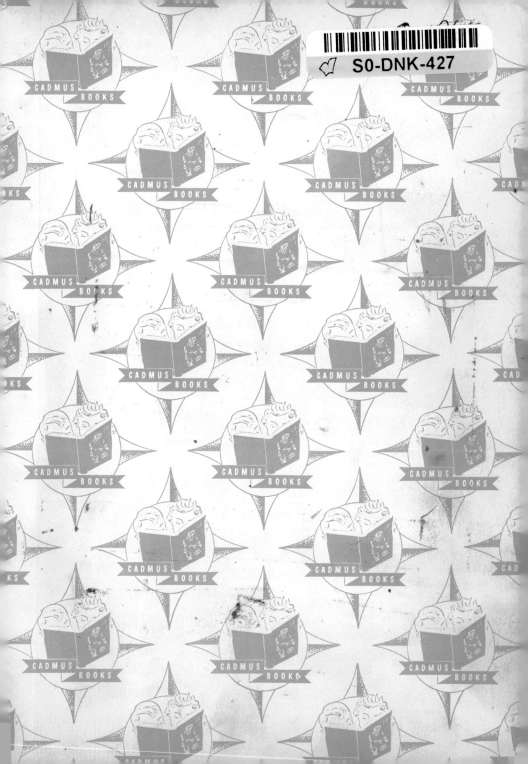

MUTT

BIANCA BRADBURY

Illustrated by Mary Stevens

1961 FIRST CADMUS EDITION
THIS SPECIAL EDITION IS PUBLISHED BY ARRANGEMENT WITH
THE PUBLISHERS OF THE REGULAR EDITION
HOUGHTON MIFFLIN CO.
BY
E. M. HALE AND COMPANY
EAU CLAIRE, WISCONSIN

MUTT

By BIANCA BRADBURY
Illustrated by MARY STEVENS

All the fancy poodles, boxers, daschunds, spaniels and collies with their ribbons won in dog shows, looked down on Mutt. Mutt didn't have any ribbons but he had lots of fun playing with Bill in the grass. But when there was a show for just plain dogs—Mutt had even more fun.

*

Dewey Decimal Classification: Fic

Mutt was just a plain dog. He belonged to Bill.

Mutt lived in an apartment house. In the next apartment lived a fancy poodle.

In the apartment next to the poodle lived a fancy cocker spaniel.

Next to the cocker spaniel lived a fancy collie.

On the OTHER side of Mutt there lived a fancy
boxer.

Next to the boxer lived a fancy dachshund.

In the last apartment on Mutt's floor, next to the
dachshund, lived a floppy, fancy Pekingese.

3

Every day these fancy dogs went for walks, on
leashes. A maid or a butler took each of them to the
park.

Every day Mutt went to the park too. But he didn't go on a leash. He ran beside Bill. They ran past all the fancy dogs. They rolled on the grass. Bill threw sticks and Mutt chased them. Mutt ran in circles and Bill chased HIM.

5

They walked home, tired and dirty and happy.

They passed the fancy dogs. The fancy dogs still looked smooth and neat. They sniffed.

The butlers sniffed.

The maids sniffed.

The poodle said to the spaniel, "What a very plain dog!"

The spaniel said to the collie, "His feet don't match. One's white and three are black!"

The collie said to the boxer, "He has burrs in his coat!"

The boxer said to the dachshund, "His tail curls up over his back!"

The dachshund said to the Pekingese, "I'm sure he hasn't a single ribbon to his name. I have four ribbons!"

The Pekingese said, "I have FIVE. I'm better than you are!"

The dogs stopped in front of the apartment house. The maids pulled. The butlers pulled. But the dogs wouldn't move.

Boxer barked, "I have EIGHT ribbons!"

Spaniel yapped, "I have TEN ribbons!"

Collie spoke last. "I've won EIGHTEEN ribbons in dog shows and I don't want to hear another yap out of any of you! I'm the best of all!"

Mutt sat on his window sill, looking down. He
heard all this. He thought, Maybe it would be nice
to have just one ribbon.

Soon after this, Mutt and Bill went to the park
as usual. They found a new sign, near the fish pool.
"Dog Show!" it said. "Next Saturday. Boys and
girls! Bring your dogs! Come and win a ribbon!"

On Saturday Bill gave Mutt a bath. He used soap.
Bill combed Mutt. He brushed him. He put a leash
on him.

They set out down the street. They passed the
six fancy dogs. The butlers and maids were steering
them away from the park.

Mutt and Bill arrived at the park. It was no won-
der the butlers and maids weren't taking their dogs
there. Dozens and dozens of dogs were milling

around on the grass. There were big dogs, little dogs, fat dogs, thin dogs, white dogs, black dogs, brown dogs, spotted dogs, yellow dogs, red dogs, fuzzy dogs, smooth dogs. There were wise dogs, silly dogs, noisy dogs, quiet dogs. There were collies, dachshunds, poodles, bird dogs, Pekingese, Scotties, bea-

gles, boxers. Some of them were fancy dogs. Maybe some of them had LOTS of ribbons at home. But they weren't yapping to brag about their ribbons. They were yapping because they were having a good time. EVERYBODY yapped. All the leashes tangled in knots.

Through the crowd came the judges. They stood in the bandstand.

They began to call boys and girls and dogs to the bandstand.

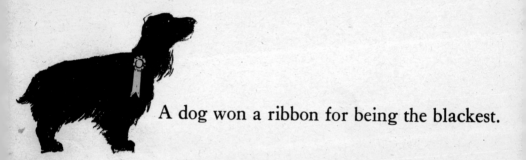

A dog won a ribbon for being the blackest.

A dog won a ribbon for being the whitest.

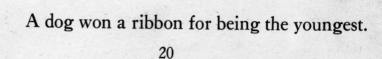

A dog won a ribbon for being the youngest.

A dog won a ribbon for being the oldest.

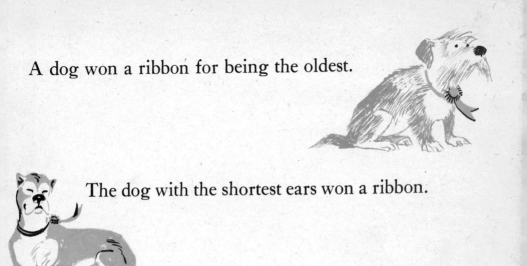

The dog with the shortest ears won a ribbon.

The dog with the longest ears won a ribbon.

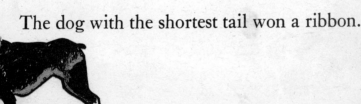

The dog with the shortest tail won a ribbon.

The dog with the longest tail won a ribbon.

Mutt was having a lovely time. He liked this dog show. Here was a whole park full of fancy dogs and just plain dogs. Everybody yapped together. There wasn't one dog sniffing down his nose at anybody else. Mutt grinned from ear to ear. He wagged his tail so hard, his tail wagged the rest of him.

Suddenly everybody looked at Bill and Mutt. A judge was calling, "You, there! You there!"

Bill pulled Mutt to the bandstand. The judge
pinned a ribbon to Mutt's collar. He shook Bill's
hand.

Bill looked at the ribbon. He read it out loud. The ribbon said, "FOR THE HAPPIEST DOG."

Bill grinned from ear to ear, now, just as Mutt was doing. "You're the happiest dog in the dog show, Mutt," he said.

He and Mutt started home.

They passed the six fancy dogs. The maids sniffed. The butlers sniffed. Mutt yapped at each dog. He stepped high. He held his head high, so that all could see his fine blue ribbon.

"What do you know?" they said. "The mutt won a ribbon!"

"Just one ribbon?" said the Pekingese. "I have FIVE ribbons!"

"I have TEN ribbons!" said the spaniel.

Now they were at it again. The butlers and the maids were tugging at them, trying to get them into the apartment house.

Mutt and Bill stepped into the elevator and rode
upstairs. They heard the growling under their window. They looked down.

There were the fancy dogs, in the street. All the leashes were tangled. All the maids and the butlers were saying cross things to each other. All the fancy dogs were saying the rudest things they could think of.

Bill put his arm around Mutt. "We won the best ribbon in the show," he said. "Did you know that, Mutt?"

Mutt could still hear the fancy dogs in the street. "I have EIGHTEEN ribbons, and I'll thank the lot of you to shut up!" the collie was barking.

Mutt wriggled with joy in Bill's arms. He didn't care if the collie had eighteen ribbons. He didn't care if the collie had eighteen HUNDRED ribbons.

He had won his ribbon for being the happiest dog of all.